Helen Cresswell has written many, many stories and has been a favourite children's author for a long time. She will be best known for the creation of *Lizzie Dripping* and *The Bagthorpe Saga* and in recent years has made several television scripts from her books, the latest being *Moondial*. Helen lives with her family in Nottinghamshire.

Frank James grew up in Fulham, London, but now lives with his wife, Claire and his two daughters in Herefordshire. He is a keen animator and enjoys learning magic tricks and photography. Before he was an illustrator, Frank worked with a boat builder and still enjoys sailing. He would like to produce children's television and build his own plane.

For Anton, Kazimir and Lukas with love.

British Library Cataloguing in Publication Data
Cresswell, Helen, *1936 –*
   Hokey pokey did it.
   I. Title   II. James, Frank
   823'.914[J]
   ISBN 0-7214-9608-3

First edition

Published by Ladybird Books Ltd Loughborough Leicestershire UK
Ladybird Books Inc Auburn Maine 04210 USA
© Text HELEN CRESSWELL MCMXC
© LADYBIRD BOOKS LTD MCMXC

Printed in England (3)

HOKEY POKEY DID IT!

by HELEN CRESSWELL
illustrated by FRANK JAMES

Ladybird Books

Sally Jemima Tidmarsh was her full name, but we'll call her Sal. Everyone else did.

She was five, and would be six next month.

Every morning Sal's mum took her to school and then went off to her job, and that was all right. Every afternoon Mum picked her up again, and that was all right.

But the minute they got home, Mum would start to cook and clean and wash, and that *wasn't* all right.

'What can I do?' Sal would wail. 'I've got nobody to play with.'

'Play with your trains,' Mum
would say. 'Go out in the
yard and skip!'

'It's no fun,' said Sal.
'Not all on my own.
Why can't I have
a brother or sister?'

'Because,' Mum said.

She always said that. It wasn't a proper answer at all.

What Sal really wanted, even more than a brother or sister, was a kitten.

Sal even dreamed about that kitten. He would be ginger, the colour of marmalade, and have big green eyes. And she would call him Hokey Pokey.

One day Sal was so tired of waiting for Hokey Pokey to arrive that she decided to play with him anyway.

'We'll play tag,' she said. 'Look out – I'm coming!'

She chased that kitten all over the room. Then, just as she touched the tip of his tail he sprang right onto the mantelpiece and – crash! Down came a blue glass jug and smashed to smithereens.

Mum rushed in from the kitchen.

'Oh, Sal!' she said. 'What have you done?'

'It wasn't me,' said Sal. She pointed at the kitten. 'Hokey Pokey did it!'

'That's a fine tale,' said Mum, and swept up the pieces.

When Mum had gone Sal ticked Hokey Pokey off. But he just purred.

Next day, Sal decided her kitten needed a bath.

'You can have it in the wash basin,' she told him. She filled it with warm water and plonked him in. He struggled and mewed and kicked his legs and soon Sal and the bathroom were very wet.

In came Mum.

'Oh, Sal!' she said. 'What a mess!'

'It wasn't me,' Sal told her. 'Hokey Pokey did it!'

'Then Hokey Pokey had better learn to behave, whoever he is!' said Mum, and mopped up the floor.

Again Sal ticked Hokey Pokey off. Again he purred.

One day the pair of them went out into the yard, looking for something to do. There was only a dustbin, a small tree and a line of washing.

'Can't catch me!'

Hokey Pokey sprang up on the dustbin and from there to the washing line. Carefully, on tiptoe, he set off along it like a tightrope walker.

'Can't catch me!'

'Oh *can't* I!'

Sal jumped. She almost touched the line. She jumped again, grabbed the line, and down it came, Hokey Pokey, washing and all.

Mum came rushing out.

'Oh, Sal – now what have you done?'

'It wasn't me,' Sal said, and pointed at the culprit. 'Hokey Pokey did it!'

'That's what you always say,' said Mum. 'Who *is* this Hokey Pokey?'

'He's invisible,' Sal said. 'He's my invisible kitten.'

Mum looked at her then, very long and hard.

'Oh, I see,' was all she said, and she started to pick up the washing.

That night Hokey Pokey slept on Sal's bed as usual.

'It's my birthday tomorrow,' she told him. 'You can come to my party and help to blow out the candles.'

He purred.

'Happy Birthday! Happy Birthday, Sal!'

Mum was drawing back the curtains.

'Hurray, I'm six!' said Sal.

'Look out of the window and see what you see!' Mum told her.

Sal stood and peered down. All she could see in the yard was a dustbin, a small tree, a clothes line and a basket with a lid.

'That's your present,' Mum said.

Sal raced downstairs. She lifted the lid of the basket. There was a kitten, a ginger one the colour of marmalade, with big green eyes.

'Hokey Pokey! Oh Mum – it's Hokey Pokey!'

And so it was. And he came to Sal's birthday party just as she had promised and helped to blow out the candles.

And after that there were no more broken jugs or soaked bathrooms or pulled down washing lines. The real Hokey Pokey was very neat and nimble on his toes.

But if ever anything *was* broken, or spilt or spoilt, Sal and her mum would look at each other and say, 'Hokey Pokey did it!' and burst out laughing.